GW01057464

La ab

ranslated from
Romansh

Blackboard
Romana Ganzoni

Translated from Romansh by
Hannah Felce

First published in English by Strangers Press, Norwich, 2022
part of UEA Publishing Project

First published by Uniun dals Grischs, 2019, as part of the
series Chasa Paterna

Printed by
Swallowtail, Norwich

Series editors
Nathan Hamilton & Lucy Rand

Editorial assistance
Lily Alden, Erin Maniatopoulou and Emma Seager

Proofread by
Senica Maltese

Cover design and typesetting
Glen Robinson (aka GRRR.UK)

Design Copyright © Glen Robinson, 2022

ISBN: 978-1-913861-47-6

Blackboard

Roberta Dapunt

Ganzoni

Translated by Hannah Felce

PART I

LA TABLA

I WAS PLEASED TO READ OF A new online venture by young Romansh voices called *La Tabla*. For me, *la tabla* is a black slate board with a wooden or plastic frame — my favourite being a frame of red plastic — on which began the most important thing to me beyond my first encounter with school and my teacher, Mr Chasper Sarott: writing. For me, writing was an extension of drawing with colours. Now I could draw with letters. Anchoring impressions and stories, describing people, their behaviour, their relationships, their secrets, their dreams, letting my mind wander and inventing alternative lives. The first notations I made were pen portraits of my classmates, when and how much they spoke, what typified them and, to this day, my class photograph remains the most important document in my story of becoming a person who writes.

When I write the word 'write' I can hear the scratch of writing chalk. I liked the harder chalk. It grated a little more on the slate – and I can see the shape of my first 'a'. My friend M. sat next to me. She had clammy hands, so was good at correcting her mistakes with her fingers. I, on the other hand, had to use a sponge. My sponge was natural, from the ocean, and if you didn't change the water, it started to stink and turned brown, even though the colour of the chalk was white. I still don't understand where the brown came from. Was it the sponge's revenge for removing it from its salty habitat to a school in the mountains to float in sweet tap water?

Sometimes the slate broke. I recall our sadistic teacher from years three and four hitting D. across the back of the head, but I'm not actually sure we still used chalkboards then. Certainly by years five and six we didn't, I don't think; the teacher for those years was just as sadistic and found other ways of humiliating the weaker pupils. The slate broke if it fell to the floor or if E. threw it like a boomerang. It seemed it broke when it had enough of this ignorant world, of all the mistakes. I remember once it had been whole when placed in my schoolbag, but when I took it out it was broken, just like that; as though just to be contrary? I continued to use it for a little while. As punishment. I ignored the cracks. I scribbled across them until I couldn't anymore.

Already, at that age, I couldn't let things go, like my chalkboard. The excitement I had for my new slate was the first thing that softened the blow. This chalkboard knew so much of me, though the pictures and the stories never had contact with it; those texts I wrote instead with a pencil in a little booklet I made with staples. It took a while for me to become accustomed to the new device; to accept it as my own.

So, how happy I am to be able to hold in my hands, so many years on, a new little blackboard, *La Tabla*, for young voices; for schoolgirls who wrote and wrote and never stopped.

PART II

SHOPPING LIST: CHEERFULNESS

Today I need to get some cheerfulness, at least two kilos for these times – and a new perspective for next year, that would be good too. I could cook it up with hope and illusion, a lot of hope and a little illusion. What do I mean a little? None! Cheerfulness, best served with cream, but not the low-fat kind, full fat, maybe even double cream, which I ate every day at university with a dessert spoon. I said two kilos of cheerfulness, didn't I? At least. And hope. How much hope do I need? Also two kilos. Don't want to overdo it, even if it is free. You can take as much as you want. You'd think that the whole world would run to the shop, but last year – a Tuesday afternoon, in May – I was the only one there. I could have taken a truckload without anyone questioning me, but I only needed enough for the following week. A couple of pinches, that was enough. And it worked. I could have used some in July, too, but I was so tired I stayed at home. It's bad when you stop going out. What else? Oh yes, this bloody perspective for next year. I'll leave it, come back later. Cheerfulness and hope will be enough for now. Perhaps the perspective will come from them if served with cream, a lot of cream.

SHOPPING LIST: WEAPONS

Weapons to fight my attackers, that's what I need today. And a
torch, a strong one, so I can see in the dark, a NiteCore LED TM36
LITE-1800 lumen. I'll buy the most expensive, at about 280 francs.
It contains a Luminus SBT-70 LED lighting module, which is much
more compact than the TM36. It's protection against exceedingly
high internal temperatures and the power automatically reduces
if it goes above 60 degrees Celsius. Which is excellent. Maybe
even a couple of matches, like the ones for lighting cigarettes, and
some long ones, too, so that I might light candles, like the ones
on Christmas trees, for my enemies. All those I've found and even
killed. They are mäuse, but they don't even know it and carry on
as normal. Only I know, I beat them, like in a video game, and in
the next round they're back. Attackers have thousands of lives.
They rise again with even more drive and strength, they are more
scheming, more subtle, wounding you with compliments. But I keep
going. One word at a time. That is my revenge.

SHOPPING LIST: DREAMS

I would like to exchange the dreams I had last night for new ones.
I'm very careful, I don't believe in complete storytelling. You cannot
direct every last detail of your dreams. Dreams take their own path,
behind the producer's back, but perhaps I could buy a box of some
that aren't so bad. I trust the new boxes I saw in the supermarket.
The label didn't describe what the dream would be, but rather what
it would not be, precisely because it wants to be a surprise. A dream
will not be dictated to. I will take the orange box that promises no
sharks and no polenta. I don't like sharks in my dreams. I do like
polenta. I have learnt you must always sacrifice something you like
to avoid something you don't. That's the deal. It hurts, but it's part
of life, my teacher said; bad things are part of life. I didn't entirely
understand. I'm still in search of a sea full of peaceful sharks whose

reputation is the only thing that's miserable and frightening, and if you look more closely, you realise it's all a misunderstanding.

SHOPPING LIST: THREE APPLES

I use the Romansh Puter 'pom' for apple rather than the Romansh Vallader 'mail'; 'mail' is too soft and postal for what I want to relate, because of the tone, I'll use 'pom': trais poms, trois pommes, bun nom.

Today I need three apples. At least three. Trais poms.

One of gold, one of silk, and one of meat.

I'll hold the golden apple in my hand and sit on a throne like a queen. I'll observe and reign. I'll reign over my house, my dogs, my cat and my saucepans, my shopping list, my time... I'll sit on my throne, observe, and reign. Fertig. The end.

I'll use the silk apple to caress myself, I'll move it along my arms, pass it to you, and play with it with my feet when it's on the floor, my toenails painted the same colour as the apple. I'll massage my face when I'm watching *Tatort*. I know that the silk will never break, because silk should be rolled and never folded, and silk on a sphere means that it will never be folded... I think of foreign lands, of Russia and the feet of ballerinas.

The apple made of meat is for eating.

Raw, with nothing else, the blood could be used as pink dye and I could smear a little on my t-shirt, so I'm left alone. I could salt my apple and roast it with a lot of rosemary. I like this herb. I could give it to someone who is starving − or eat it myself. I could let this apple rot and enjoy the smell of putrefying flesh without having to be dead, how alive that might make me feel.

SHOPPING LIST: A SUITCASE

I want a circus suitcase, one into which you can disappear and come out wherever you want, like Genoa. I'll climb into the suitcase and come out in the Stanza della Poesia on Piazza Matteotti. I'll be

holding a poem, one I wrote but is not entirely my own, which came
from itself, the one about the beggar. Or the text in which I roam
the streets pickpocketing moments... *Essere a Genova per non
far alcuna esperienza, per premunirmi contro le esperienze... nella
speranza che altri possano fare tutte le esperienze e che io possa
leggerle in essi... come ringraziamento per la loro fatica di vivere,
e non vorrei dimenticare nessuno.*[1] Or the text in which I see lions
everywhere, not only in front of the Duomo San Lorenzo; even the
neighbour's dog in the Palazzo dei Giustiniani is a lion... I'm there
now giving a reading, the people who are always there are there
too, the regulars, even the young guy who put a poem in my bag
that says how words change every hour... Maybe I'm holding a text
in which the suitcase that is now on my shopping list was invented.
Because inventions are not human, because they come from a
different realm, far away, you might sometimes want to buy your
own. But we receive them as gifts — we don't deserve them, but
receive them nonetheless.

SHOPPING LIST: MUSHROOMS FOR MY MOTHER

Next on my shopping list are mushrooms for my mother, if I can find
a greengrocer who has the right ones. They must have particular
attributes. They need to be the size of melons, watermelons, and
they must be plantable in the forest, up by Tschlin, down by Sur
En, at Avrona, towards S-charl, there, where it's straight, where it's
level (on the Bödali, the plain), there, where my mother collected
mushrooms for decades, while her eyes were still good.

Collecting mushrooms was her first passion, and I admired the
fire that drove her to the forest. Like a hungry animal, she wandered
her favourite spots, secret territories. I couldn't walk when she took
me the first time, so she placed me under a beautiful larch before
starting her rounds. Each round she moved further away, calling
Romaliiii, Romaliiii over and over to calm me. It meant 'I haven't
forgotten you, daughter, but I have things to do.' I was very happy,

because I could have natural yoghurt with grated apple, to this day one of the best things a person can eat. I loved that my mother followed her passion. Having such parents means they don't bother you all the time. When I'm writing, I do my rounds, from time to time calling out my children's names, or to my husband...

---

[1] 'Being in Genoa not to have an experience, but to guard against experiences... in the hope that others can have all the experiences and I can read those experiences in them... as thanks for their effort to live, I would endeavour not to forget any one of them.'

PART III

THE BOX OF SIX WONDERS I

There is an Engadin fairy tale about Maria and the three witches, written by Gian Bundi and told by Nann'Engel. [2] The first witch is named Elisabetta Travers, the second, Elisabeth, and the third, Elisa, which means: one Elisabeth with the strength of three, and sharp teeth. She has an aunt with even sharper teeth who has a box, the Box of Six Wonders, stolen from the good. The box contains:

✳ Maria
✳ A red silk ribbon, used to wrap presents, like the one Maria follows to
✳ a magic trapdoor, behind which she finds
✳ a narrow marble staircase that leads to hidden worlds
✳ A beautiful big lounge, it's cosy there, but Maria is trapped
✳ George who slays every dragon
✳ Their kiss
✳ A calming cup of coffee
✳ Two biscuits on a plate. Sweet, like Maria and George
✳ George's gold wand. The secret between them, magic.
✳ An egg – maybe Fabergé – a treasure made of enamel and diamonds, like the gift for Maria from George, like love.
✳ A lake. The good can drink its clean water, the bad drown in murky waves.
✳ A saw, made of gold, to saw away the witches' balcony so they too drown.
✳ A fairy tale of three witches.

THE BOX OF THE SIX WONDERS II

So have you heard the Engadin fairy tale about the three witches? The first witch, Elisabetta Travers, the second, Elisabeth, and the third, Elisa, which means: one Elisabeth with the strength of three. A powerful woman with sharp teeth. She has an aunt with even sharper teeth who owns the Box of Six Wonders. Do you want to know what's in the box? It contains:

* The ring your mother wore when her hand was still young. The one you loved and she lost many years ago. Here it is, found.
* Your singing voice in the first year of school.
* A letter you couldn't write. All the things you couldn't say.
* The shoes you didn't have the courage to buy. The ones with green dots.
* The neighbour's dog.
* All the well-meaning glances you missed.

THE BOX OF THE SIX WONDERS III

What could be in the Box of Six Wonders? I'll tell you:

The World of Water: On Christmas morning, standing in your bathroom, you spit out the rest of the toothpaste and look in the mirror. Your crooked nose doesn't bother you. It has character. Your hair doesn't shine, but you're not an advert for L'Oréal either. You use the fancy sample shampoo nicked from the posh hotel. You want a healthy lather while you sing.

The second wonder: The World of the Midday Air. You're sitting on the roof of your house daydreaming, then you jump and you're flying with all the other people. Some of them you know; one's a total misery who never greets others when he passes by. You see each other differently now. He always thought the misery was you.

The World of Earth: Your garden. Plants that don't usually grow in the mountains grow there in December. Hydrangeas and lemons. You pick them and know everything about each one.

Towards evening: The World of Fire. You won't believe it, but out of the box springs your kitchen and somehow you know how to cook like a French God. You're cooking complicated sauces, you know all the recipes par coeur, your favourite Christmas pudding is cooking in the oven.

The World of Love: It's night. You're in your bed. And you feel loved. It's underneath you like a pillow, it's over you like a quilt. You smell like rare perfume. You've dreamt, flown, the cake was delicious, next to you is a bouquet of blue hydrangeas.

The box is the box is the box. The six wonders *are* the box.

---

2 The fairy tale is about Maria, who follows a red ribbon through a trap door to a room, which turns out to be a witches' lair and she is captured by the three witches and made to do chores to avoid being eaten. She has a visitor, George, who magically appears. He helps Maria with her chores in exchange for a cup of coffee, a biscuit, and a kiss. After he helps her several times, he advises Maria to steal the box from the witches' aunt when they send her to collect the Box of Six Wonders. George gives Maria a magic egg, which cracks open when she throws it on the floor during her escape. A big lake appears in which the aunt drowns, because she is evil. While Maria makes her escape, George makes sure the three witches drown in the lake too. They then live happily ever after.

PART IV

ROSY CHEEKS

They've stopped at Landquart. The twelve-year-old informs his mother that his classmate bought a jumper from Polo Ralph Lauren, dark blue, simple, super cool. He wonders whether this shopping outlet, this shopping 'village', full of offers, brands, labels; full of luxury products (mass-produced, darling, his mother corrects) is in Landquart. He thinks it's in Landquart.

The mother isn't interested. No idea, she says. I think these places are a shame, she says. Pure consumerism, she says. They want to keep the shops open on 24th December, even if it falls on a Sunday, she says. What a shame, she repeats. A real shame. And classic jumpers like that are for boring people, she says. And by the way, don't say 'super cool', understood?

Her son lowers his gaze. Do you want a sandwich, she asks. I brought them with me. Vegan cheese on granary bread. Do you want one? No thanks, he says and takes out a bag full of multicoloured gummi bears. His mother wrinkles her nose. Those aren't healthy, she says. Oh, well, he responds. Each to their own, says the mother.

They change trains in Chur.

The mother gets up, she has needed to go to the bathroom since Sargans. She moves quickly, the need seems great. The boy smirks. The mother runs. Five minutes pass. Ten minutes. Twenty.

The boy follows the direction his mother took, looking for the loo. The first he finds locked, but above the keyhole he can clearly see the green square. Strange. The conductor has hung a sign that reads 'Defekt – Out of Order – Fuori servizio', underneath, some joker has scribbled 'Piss at home!' The boy takes his pen out of his backpack and adds 'hahaha'.

Nevertheless, someone seems to be sitting in the toilet that is fuori servizio. Is that a kid's voice? Hey youuu, the boy calls. No answer.

Having walked through the next two carriages, the boy knocks energetically on the toilet door in first class. Don't stress, says his mother. She laughs.

I was worried you'd got off the train at Thusis, Mum, says the boy and makes his way back to their seats. After a long while – the train now in Tiefencastel – his mother returns, a little dishevelled, her cheeks rosy, and asks, What's happening with this jumper? You won't find Polo Ralph Lauren in Landquart. They'd likely have to go to Fox Town, in Mendrisio, they could go next weekend, if the boy wanted. You could use a new jumper, couldn't you?

The boy stares up at his mother and shakes his head. And now she's starving, a nice steak, that would be great right now, super cool. There's a restaurant car on the train. Come, let's go, she says. He collects his things and follows. In a good mood now, the mother laughs out loud as she plucks an orange gummi bear from the boy's packet.

THE LITTLE CORAL TREE

Years ago, Nina's godmother, whom she had always admired, gave her an exquisite coral brooch. It diverts harmful gazes, she'd said. Gazes that might wish you harm — the malocchio. There's an Italian proverb 'non tutto il male viene per nuocere', not all bad things cause harm. 'Harm' comes from the Old English 'hearm', to hurt.

Nina, who generally feared a lot of things, wanted to believe. Since you cannot know the future, or who or what might be there to help or to harm, it's best to remain vigilant. So why not wear a beautiful piece of jewellery, thought Nina, who anyway liked to dress up and adorn herself with pretty things.

The brooch was from a strong and rigid coral tree from Sardinia. It was blood-red coral, Mediterranean coral. Her godmother had said it was the only thing strong enough to fight the malocchio.

It wasn't clear to Nina how this protection might work. Is this spiky little tree so complicated to look at that it might absorb all their attention, suck the strength from their bones and souls? Do the gazes of evil people somehow fumble around and snag in its branches, side to side, up and down, and get lost? By this theory, presumably people who might wish harm on others could only be directionless and stupid. If only such things were true.

Sadly, malevolence remains unlinked to a person's cognitive or intellectual potential, rather to other forces Nina did not want to explore; it was more than enough to know what harm there is in the world, what humans are capable of doing to others — even if modern psychology often considered aggressors the real victims. She did not want to worry about the motives of these crimes, especially not as a potential victim herself. If someone had decided to give her the malocchio, it was likely to have already been too late.

Nina wore the brooch every day on her chest, right beside her heart.

She did not want to forgive a person who had willed her to break a leg or lose her purse, or who had willed her dead. She would wish instead that the aggressor break a leg or lose their purse as a result of their own action (but would not wish death on anyone, that would be unlucky). She hoped the little coral tree would reflect and toss back the other person's evil. That it might work like Perseus's mirror against Medusa; that the person with such negative thoughts might stand there instead surprised, petrified, reprimanded.

What if, Nina asked herself, after an unusually strange meeting and phone call with her godmother, the woman whom I admire the most might reveal *herself* to be the person who wishes me harm? What if she put all her hate into my 'protection'? My godmother, with her regal, obscure, worldly aura, who has been my idol for years. What then?

Nina worried, as she caressed the brooch, as she repeatedly opened and closed the old silver clasp, until one day it broke. That should have been a moment to reconsider. For her to take seriously the thought that this little clasp, which kept the protective brooch on her blouse over her heart, was in fact the door latch on a trojan horse of doubt and bad luck invading her.

Nina had the smith attach a brand-new pin and clasp made of pure gold, 18 carats, for 450 francs.

Then one day in summer the brooch fell to the ground and Nina stepped on it and accidentally broke it into many pieces. At first, she was devastated, but after a few seconds a feeling of joy overcame her. She felt relieved. She did not know why. Still, Nina picked up every piece of the red coral, putting each away in a small velvet bag with the intention of getting it fixed soon. But she never did.

THE TRIP

Day 1: Two stops away on the metro. Thousands of people. Or more. There, mothers have to wash their children with mineral water, the weather doesn't always allow for bathing in the streets. The children are crying. I don't hear their cries. I'm standing below an orange tree and hear the man standing next to me talking into his mobile phone made of gold. The children's voices are not strong enough to make such a journey. Two stops away on the metro can be a long way.

Day 2: Today they announced the road had been cleared, that they had cleared the road of refugees, with soap. But I don't smell the road or the soap, I'm standing beneath a tree that's carrying oranges, it's full, they look like Christmas baubles. Soon the tree will flower. Neroli. Its perfume will diffuse everywhere. It's a scent that raises the spirits. At least there, when it blooms, at least for a moment. At least for some people.

Day 3: Beggars. Men, women and children. Drug users, the poor, and those better off than they let on. Faces change when someone approaches asking for money. Many are from here, but some are from other countries too. They play music or wait on the side of the road, they walk around collecting change. I don't know if they look me in the eye, because I don't look them in the eye. I look at their forehead or their nose, give them a euro, stare at the ground.

Day 4: They said there had been a protest two or three weeks ago. Apparently, thousands of lawyers and judges came to the capital to protest; they hardly earn a thing. It seems that they came in their civil gowns and hung their collars on the branches of a tree, which now competes with the orange trees that decorate the roads. The one here, where I am, is magnificent, but you shouldn't eat its fruits, they say, because they're poisonous. Because of the traffic. Many cars pass by, Mini Coopers in all colours possible. People who aren't poor no longer have the courage to drive around in their big cars. I also have a Mini Cooper at home. It's blue.

Day 5: In this country, you drink espresso cold. The waiter mixes the coffee with ice and shakes it in a metal shaker until there's a nice white foam, he then fills the glass and serves. What a drink! The customer is me. I'm sitting on the terrace of the Acropolis

Museum, observing the island of temples in the centre of the city.
My life is a single Sunday at midday. I take a sip of cold espresso
and think of Aphrodite's hardly visible face. There is a single point
of oxidisation on the marble that makes it look like the goddess is
crying black tears.

SONNTAG & SOHN, LEIPZIG

Sonntag & Sohn. Jewellers. Established 1897 in Leipzig, where
Goethe studied law. It's on the rise again; the city is hip, vibrant.
Engagement rings shine through their window, with smaller pieces,
silver pieces, lighter on the wallet. Beside them sit little earrings with
rubies and sapphires in reds and blues, gilded chains, heavy clasps,
gold, diamonds, intimate pieces, pieces as brilliant as the sun or
stars, as though they might retain the poetry of the firmament were
the sun and stars to disappear, pieces that soak up emotion, if the
gloves are removed, the jumper, the blouse, the shirt, because they
dare to touch the skin.

It always feels like Sunday morning near Sonntag & Sohn,
perhaps because they're a duo: father and son, Sunday and
Saturday, a summer weekend. A quiet, constant strength of loyalty
born of successful history, that says: family means something, Blut
ist dicker als Wasser, blood is thicker than water, even today, in
2017, a time that feels like it wants everything reinterpreted anew.
Sonntag & Sohn still feels set in an earlier time of reassurance
and sandwiches, butter, jam and coffee. Sonntag & Sohn says: the

midday canons are quiet, it's Sunday, people go to church, like in a French film from the sixties; people go for a walk, the women wear their best pearl necklaces, life's as good as it's ever been.

Sunday and daughter. What kind of business might that be? What would they sell in that shop? Is Sonntag's son perhaps a Monday after all, and Sunday's daughter the only Saturday? A weekend for mothers and daughters. Evenings by the river or lake? A relationship that doesn't require them to be best friends; to have the same jean size or require Sunday to wear ripped jeans like an insult to all who are broke and try to keep their clothing in good order.

Sunday and daughter are in their motor and sail boat factory seven days a week, with eight hundred female workers. Their fingers smell of iron, wood and paint. They don't say much. They don't have a private life. In July, they have one week's holiday in Leipzig. It's tradition, the only fun they have all year. The rest of the time they work.

THE FUR COAT

There's a fur shop in Zurich at 208 Freiestrasse that has been there for decades. Years ago, a famous stylist used to languor glamorously in the ground floor rooms, now full of coats, jackets, pillows, bags, hats, and sofa throws. Andy Warhol is supposed to have once visited and I picture the stylist wearing white boots like Diana Rigg as Emma Peel in *The Avengers*. She has an oversized leopard-print jacket and the gaze of an oriental princess; a gaze that somehow imbued upon the space such an elegance of the seventies that it had to one day be a fur shop.

And for decades now you've had to walk past offcuts of fur coats to get to the apartments above; coats made of wolf fur, mink fur, chinchilla fur, rabbit fur, beaver fur, coats made of all kinds of furry things. There's even the tail of an ocelot — possibly an offcut from the floor-length coat worn by German Hannelore M., wife of Dr. M. (through which she automatically gained a title:

Mrs. Dr. M.) in Scuol and in Vulpera when I was a child. I would call after this immense woman: 'Hey, no killing!', which just made her laugh and she would sway like a Corinthian column, topped with an immense undulation of blonde hair. Hair so blonde it brought to mind Rumpelstiltskin, who must surely have spun gold from straw for her too; a Venus draped in fur bought at half price from a shop in Düsseldorf West. Or perhaps Mrs. Dr. M. only rented the ocelot fur and next year, it'll be a baby lion's skin she'll use to swan around Switzerland, with the hairdos and golden personalities of the old Nazis they both were, while driving their green Mercedes to St. Moritz.

Upon entry, as you walk past the ocelot's tail, the offcuts of wolf and other furs, the effect is a blend of great sensuality, of a soft luxuriousness that makes you want to touch and smell, and a morbid sensation of being surrounded by the cadavers and the suffering of creatures without voice or language. As if the beauty of the material were supposed to justify it, as it tells of a history of humanity and of human nature; of this creature at once a small and gentle mammal that might lick your hand, and a wild, aggressive, starving, greedy, depraved, animal that sometimes kills as a game, like a cat; both angel and demon, a creature that might kill another creature, skin it, and tear off its flesh to drape around its own shoulders, believing it makes them fast and strong; that might eat or just throw away the flesh; that might be proud of its actions, or guilty or ashamed. Walking past the furs is like taking hot and cold showers, an oscillation or vibration like a meaning between an assortment of ambiguous things.

My husband and I rented the apartment on the second floor. It was for our son and ideal for a shared student flat. I could already see the fridge full of Calanda Bräu. Before that, I was able to use the rooms to write. For six weeks above the fur shop, every day I would sit at the kitchen table with an odour of fur in my nostrils. It gave my coffee an entirely different taste. Everything tasted different, more intense than at home, but also more bitter.

FOR NOTHING

I am waiting for the bus, number 31, at Hegibachplatz in Zurich. It is morning and time for a snack. It is November, a typical day in November, or how you'd imagine a typical day in November to be. It is foggy, it is damp. People look at their own shoes or stare into their phones. Everyone is silent. Why isn't anyone whistling? I realise I haven't heard anyone whistle in a long time and I miss it. Should I whistle? Frère Jacques, something like that? Some are pacing to and fro, a little boy does a little hop, an old lady is sitting on a bench holding her shopping bag close. Drivers don't like to stop at the yellow lines on the road that allow pedestrians to cross. The florist's, 'Blumenhaus Hegibach', has less choice in its shop window than usual. White roses, poppies, poinsettias. And in my bag is a rather unhappy book, one that I need to read for a review. I can feel it kicking and complaining.

The Forch tram passes, heading the wrong way up towards the Rehalp cemetery. It's a beautiful cemetery, like a park. Barbara, my friend with the two dogs, Agathe and Joy, is buried there. She used to live at Hegibachplatz at the same time I did with my husband and our first child, a little boy, some twenty years ago. Our apartment faced the Neumünsterpark, an idyllic place with a sequoia tree, a species which arrived in Europe at the end of the nineteenth century, at the same time as the one growing at the Sprecherhaus in Maienfeld, and the two in Soglio, in the Baroque garden behind Palazzo Salis. I heard someone dropped a cigarette near one of those beautiful twin trees, and now one of them is dying.

When I think of Soglio, I think of Charlotte von Salis, who died recently, mother of Katharina von Salis, the natural scientist who lives in the Upper Engadin. Charlotte made a lasting impression on me, thirty years ago. I had a job entering all the Sprecherhaus library data into the computer. Charlotte had come to Maienfeld to research the sequoia tree and acquaint herself more generally with the gardens of Grisons. Helena von Sprecher was still alive at that time, another grande dame who left this world for a better one a long time ago. Women of such character. Unforgettable women.

When I'm at Hegibachplatz, I think of Barbara. I think of her often, like when I'm cooking – she was an excellent cook – but also when I need a retort to fend someone off with speed, but also charm and kindness. Barbara was an Austrian who had emigrated to Brazil, but then ultimately landed in Bülach because her husband, a Brazilian, was a pilot (captain) for Swissair at the time. Barbara's husband was very dominant, and their eventual divorce was a disaster. And later, her youngest son took his own life in a psychiatric clinic. But Barbara never gave up. What spirit she had! Humour, heart, soul. Even though she had financial and other worries, even when the weather was normal for November, or she was in pain, she would say: Was für ein wunderbarer Tag! What a wonderful day!

During her funeral in the chapel at the Rehalp cemetery, a butterfly landed near me on the wall. Its wings were patterned with the red of Barbara's hair and it had landed in a sunny spot and was still. I thought: Barbara, is that really you? Isn't this a little cliché, a little tasteless, Barbara, to appear as a butterfly in a chapel at your own funeral? I heard her laugh, out loud, her low and sonorous laugh, and I thought of how she'd said she wanted to be buried with two lit Marlboro cigarettes between her teeth. She wanted a huge coffin and to be dressed up like the diva she was. To this day, I still ask myself why they had to stuff her into one of those miserable urns. Barbara laughs about that too. She shakes her head and says: Das ist doch piepegal. Who gives a shit.

The Forch tram passed in the direction of the cemetery and Zollikerberg. Time is going slowly. How long have I been waiting for this bloody tram? Nearly half an hour? Has there been an accident? Is the loudspeaker broken? Some people have already set off in the direction of Stadelhofen on foot. Luckily in the city there aren't bus or tram accidents involving people – Personenunfälle, suicides – like there are on the Swiss Federal Railway lines. I've even experienced those kinds of tragedies on the line between Chur and Zurich. At least I don't have to brace myself for such a thing here. I'm standing on my tiptoes. The thought of Barbara has me wanting to move around.

It would have been more sensible to walk down towards Kreuzplatz. It wouldn't have hurt to move my legs, I've become a real couch potato, spending my days sitting in front of my laptop, waiting at the supermarket checkout, or for the number 31 bus with everyone else. I look at the tips of my toes, at my black shoes, the chunky ones with a heel, the leather at the front scuffed a little, the polish no longer able to hide that they were cheap, bought at Dosenbach for 69 francs, 90. The soles are a right mess. I wouldn't tell anyone but I like them best out of all my shoes, and I wear them the most often. Barbara says: Billig heisst nicht schlecht. Cheap doesn't mean bad.

The bus still isn't here. I decide to walk towards Kreuzplatz. As I set out a blonde woman next to me starts talking into her mobile phone. Forty-five minutes of my life wasted, for nothing! she complains. Barbara's eyes widen. Mine too. *For nothing*? The waiting is all for nothing? No, I don't believe that.

PART V

THE CINEMA

The cinema was in the town hall. Mrs. Anni sold Coca Cola and, most importantly, Frisco cornettos. It didn't feel like you had been to the cinema if you hadn't had an ice cream.

There was one showing a week. Often the same people gathered there on a Saturday, people who were dependent on these stories, or rather, on Hollywood. Films d'auteurs weren't really a thing then. Or at least not for me, I was certainly no critic.

It wasn't just about the love stories or the thrillers and the tension, or about the plot; it was that the cinema brought the world to the village, too – and that it's like that everywhere. The cinema brought the world to London. Films showed Scuol how things worked in New York, Ohio and Brazil. And, at the same time, the cinema revealed how things worked in tiny little Tschlin. Where there's a cinema and a library, there's no excuse for small-mindedness.

And it's not just about watching the films, it's about watching the people too. I remember how B. laughed far too loudly when the cat was killed in *Midnight Express*. I was sitting in the third row, and he was right behind me. From then on, I knew I had to watch out for that guy.

THE CARPENTER'S WORKSHOP

The Roners owned a carpenter's workshop. It was a long wooden building, a pretty imposing shed. Out front, there was a machine that cut tree trunks and looked like it was spitting out boards. Inside, it was loud and I had a lot of respect for the carpenters because, unlike me, they appeared to be focused. They had to know what they were doing, otherwise it wouldn't be long before they lost a part of a finger, or a whole hand.

The workshop was located between the school and Chasa Staila, where my friend D. lived. Sometimes we would walk home together. She walked very slowly. We used to stop for a break on the little bridge and she always had a lot to say, which I liked. She had theories. I thought a lot less than she did.

My parents' ski shop was near the workshop. If I was at the shop before six thirty, I could go home in the car.

To this day, I'm still wandering around with a friend, collecting things to give as gifts, daydreaming; I still like to go to restaurants until midnight like old times and then be driven home by car.

It was already mid-winter by the time I went to get some more sawdust from the Roners' to fill my hamster Tutu's cage. In Romansh, a hamster is called a 'raspader', or 'furmanter', but no one has use for these words anymore.

THE BAKERY

My godfather, Friedel, owned a bakery. The Schlatter bakery; rolls, doughnuts, pastries, chocolate, and ample pan cun paira, Engadin pear loaves, all the time... My godfather and his wife, Gisela, ran two shops, one on the main road and one down on Dualatscha, which housed the oven. Gisela was a person for whom time spread out, like an ocean. She was never in a hurry, which was good for the confections, they also needed time and calm.

I respected that a baker needs to wake up very early, at four in the morning. To be one of the only people up working at night and sleeping during the day was mysterious. Like occupying a different, but parallel world. Perhaps Friedel would chat to Bischoff the blacksmith on the phone just to pass the time? Did they talk about their lives, make plans for when they eventually retired, at a hundred years old? Or did they not talk at all, simply worked away in their separate, private worlds?

A Pfünderli Schwarzbrot, a pound of dark rye, that's what my mother used to ask for and what I had to say whenever I went for bread. I can't remember how much it cost back then. I have never tasted such bread since. The same is true for Vintschgauerli, Friedel's speciality – or Engadinerli, as it's known in Zurich. It's a moist rye I still like best with a slice of Bündnerfleisch.

Another gift from the mountains.

THE GARAGE

The Pfister garage was a sacred place because of Linard Pfister. The kindest man in Scuol, I was allowed to call him Uncle Linard and I wanted to go to the garage often, to where it smelled of petrol and oil and to where tools, cars and parts were scattered all over the place. There was usually a mechanic laid out working under a car and the worker from Tyrol would be swearing. He was a laid-back guy, like the boss.

Uncle Linard would lift me up when I went to visit. You 'sparrow', he'd call me when I was up high over his head. He seemed then at least ten metres tall and as if he weighed 250 kilos and could throw me some 120 metres up into the air. I felt like I must only weigh a few grams and like I could touch the sky, which I imagined had the texture of blotting paper. That texture has likely changed, it's been a long time since I had occasion to touch it. Since he died, I've felt like I no longer could or wanted to anyway.

His wife was the most beautiful of all the women, of course, and they had three daughters who were allowed to watch television in the afternoon and a dog that would follow me home once his owner had placed me back on the ground, because he was free to do so. Because he hadn't yet been put on a lead.

THE BUTCHERS

The Bierts' butchers in Scuol stank of blood. There were pigs' heads all over the ceiling and they peered down at the customers and the children waiting for another slice of baloney that made you want to remain a child forever. The shop was small and narrow. The owners, too, were small, but not narrow. The wife's hair was always coiffured, as was considered the proper do for a businesswoman at the time. Even the gardener's wife used hair rollers, as did my mother, who would soon be a businesswoman too − my parents were to rent the place next door for their ski shop. It had piggy wallpaper and the pigs would stay for the first season, before disappearing under a white layer of Pavatex.

The butcher hired by the Bierts was a tall man with an immense stomach and a wild look in his eye. I often had the sense that he carried various knives under his snow-white apron spattered with red stains. His kingdom was meat, which shone in the centre of little white plates that weren't always clean.

THE BLACKSMITHS

The Blacksmiths on Vih was like the laboratory of either Hephaestus or the devil or both. Perhaps they did their apprenticeship in Scuol, or worked hand in hand with Jachen Bischoff, the blacksmith of legend who worked day and night and must only occasionally have slept and even then standing up. For five minutes. In the evening. Between a hammer and an anvil, a rock and a hard place. Maybe he lay down on the anvil on a Sunday.

In front of the shop there were gates, metallic bits and bobs, and other beautiful junk that would be hammered and hewn into objects of such delicate aesthetic touch it was hard to believe they had anything to do with the grumpy guy who could often be heard shouting and swearing from outside. If the door to the blacksmiths was open, you could see him with hammer in his hand working with such force that sometimes it looked like the sparks were flying out of his ears. I didn't dare look too closely. I had respect for this place, which seemed to keep the whole village warm, that held back the snow queen who might otherwise freeze the whole village, the whole valley still and white like a blank page. It is said that with his hammering Bischoff forged the beat for the Engadin choirs. Perhaps for all the choirs of this world.

THE BAR

Returning from kindergarten in the afternoons, I would pass Milo Bigler's Sporthotel on the main road. My dad's red business car with the white writing was often parked there at that time. When I saw it, my mouth would start watering at the thought of the scoop of strawberry ice cream I'd get at the regulars' table, served in a golden bowl.

If I was lucky, I'd get driven home in the car too. It always felt like an adventure. Dad wouldn't speak much. And when he did, he'd comment mainly just on what he was doing, the tricks to changing gears, steering. I wasn't alone in thinking no one else drove as well as he did. He was firmly of the opinion himself, too, and would accept all praise as a well-deserved ovation.

In the middle of the round regulars' table was an octagonal ashtray with an ibex on it. Four or five men were usually sat around it, and normally around half of them were drunk. Their beers were a pretty shade of amber. Sometimes there was shouting. I liked it when the men argued. If my Dad was caught up in it, I would ask, amidst the commotion, if I could have a second scoop of ice cream, or a raspberry coulis, and he would answer with jo jo, yeah yeah, because he needed his energy for the tussle.

PART VI
C H R I S T M A S

LONDON

Searching for Christmas. In London city centre. During the last week of Advent. Piccadilly Circus. Baubles everywhere like huge apples, a dark and festive red like the apples M. used to bring to school. They were presents, given every year after her family had been to the market in Tirano. Because of this, Tirano has always seemed to me a friendly and generous place.

M.'s apples were shaped almost like pears and were a red that made you think of fairy tales, of Snow White, of her blood, a deeper red than any other blood; because such fairy-tale blood is very red. Like fairy-tale black is very black, like the white is whiter than paper.

But M.'s weren't apples for Snow White, who anyway would never again take a bite so readily. Instead, if she could have seen one of these apples from Tirano, which her stepmother would likely have bought from M., she would have polished it with a silk handkerchief, perhaps one kept as a keepsake from her real mother.

That's how it was for me. I would never eat one of M.'s apples straight away. It was too exotic a treasure, too perfect, and I would sometimes keep it so long it became mealy, until it had lost all flavour, could no longer live up to its yearly promise. Like Christmas.

PARIS

Round and round goes the three-tiered carousel, near Galeries Lafayette with its Haussmann dome and where a huge Christmas tree has been erected, one of the ones that looks almost like a stuffed animal. I've bought three rides so far and I'm sitting on a black horse I've named Sandokan, because I was in love with Sandokan when I was a girl of nine or ten.

Sandokan was a pirate who fought for justice on the island of Malaysia and it was Christmas when *The Tiger of Malaysia*, with his bright green eyes, appeared on television. It was the same two years earlier with *Arpad der Zigeuner*. I idolised these characters and saw myself not as their wife or partner but as a kind of female counterpart. Nomad, fighter, free.

Sandokan fought against the British colonists; Arpad, a Hungarian Robin Hood of sorts, fought for the Romani against the Austrians. The French actor, Robert Etcheverry, became famous as Arpad and died here, in Paris, in 2007, in November ten years ago. Perhaps somewhere near this three-tiered carousel.

I'm sitting on my black horse and have two rides left. Round and round we go.

GENOA

Christmas has not come to the port. Condoms float along with McDonald's packaging and other rubbish in the water. A beggar is talking into his hand as if it's a mobile phone. The hand is apparently impudent and won't stop arguing back. He's shouting at his hand and, annoyed, he kicks the wall painted with a big laughing monkey holding a skull like an imperial apple. The air smells like focaccia and onions.

I am hungry for pesto, but it's morning and you don't eat pesto in the morning, you drink coffee, but still, here I am, hungry for pesto. I take my book out of my red bag and start to read. I'm sitting on the stairs in front of the Duomo San Lorenzo. A stone lion stands guard.

On my left hand, I'm wearing my aunt's ring, zia Giulia Klainguti, the last Klainguti of Genoa. Today, only one remaining pâtisserie carries her name. It's nearby, five minutes by foot. The café has roasted almonds and confectionery and the shabby chic quality that tourists have come to expect. Maybe I'm a tourist, though I have no expectations here. I didn't expect this ring either, but here it is – her heirs gave it to me.

I know Giulia would have wanted me to wear it, so that's what I'm doing here now: look at my hand. The diamond flower sits on my ring finger like it's a throne. On my index finger, I'm wearing a golden skull. His name is Ottokar and you can move his jaw. A Baroque pair that speak not only of Christmas, but also of death.

ZURICH

The perfect Christmas is celebrated with Sprüngli ice fruits. The perfect Christmas is the one with the picture-perfect Christmas tree, cream-coloured baubles, a cream-coloured silk garland and fashionably traditional food. Half the city has bought it in ready-prepared, but the lady of the house still does a little, oversees the oven for example, because that's chic.

The guests act picture-perfect like guests invented by American TV, but today, today I'm my own invention of bad taste. Children are used as decoration. They are expected to sing and jump for joy as they unwrap their mountain of plastic. From the New Testament, the Story of Christmas is read aloud and forms the central subject of today's picture-perfect content. A child was born and poverty doesn't stink so much in the living room above Lake Zurich. All is palatable. All is calm. The goose is ready and stuffed with organic apples. The goose isn't organic, the organic ones were sold out.

So is this made of plastic, asks a child who should hold his tongue. He gawps at the pile of presents, that's enough! He sings with the voice of an angel, that's enough! He's running around, that's enough! The picture-perfect tree shall be knocked over, onto the lady of the house and her husband and the perfect pictures of the picture-perfect couple with the picture-perfect Christmas shall fall from the wall, and the picture-perfect house shall start to burn and all shall sink and drown in Lake Zurich. That's my Christmas wish. I think it profoundly Christian.

CHUR

My Nana used to shop at Disam, a jewellers in Chur. Like Nana, it's no longer around. She bought and repaired everything there. For example, her opal earrings that changed colour depending on your mood, so she said. If you're angry, the opal knows. As a result, I feared this stone. I still don't like opals in my ears. I don't want others to know my mood, especially if I don't myself know whether I am angry or sad. Still, the earrings would know, and a stranger on the bus or on the train or in the street might remark firmly, I know you're sad, I can see it. I might deny it. 'B-b-but I'm not sad', I might say to the stranger, but they would always know better.

What remains of my Nana is the energy of her language. A momentum and depth that no longer exists. I look for her language on my keyboard, in stories, poems and dreams. Her letters: burnt, thrown away, put in the paper basket and gone.

Discarding these letters did us a great disservice. Her language is retained in my mother, in me, in my daughter. I search for proverbs and Nana's laughter at the end of a well-executed sentence, to capture her strength, her impudence.

I hold here the little gold necklace from Disam, which I received one Christmas, years ago. It shines like a word in my Nana's voice which shone like her golden blonde hair.

PART VII

PATRIOTISM AND SUFFICIENCY
The Buildings of Gonda

The first Chasa Paterna was released in 1920 with the title *Las chasas da Gonda*.[3] It cost 50 raps. Rosa Saluz from Lavin, one of the creators of the Chasa Paterna series, wrote the story. Fifty-two pages of love and war set in the middle of the Grisons Turmoil,[4] amidst the to and fro of the Franco-Venetian alliance and the Spanish Habsburgs, between Protestants and Catholics, man and woman, between May 1618 and May 1621.

---

[3] The Chasa Paterna is the book series published by the regional Uniun dals Grischs, a union engaged with the linguistic and cultural promotion and maintenance of the Ladin dialects of Romansh, spoken in the Engadin, Val Müstair and Bergün. The title of the first edition of the Chasa Paterna is translated as *The Buildings of Gonda*.

[4] The Grisons Turmoil, the contest over the ownership of the Alpine passes in Grisons as part of the Thirty Years' War, led to a period of austerity in the Engadin. Many of the villages were devastated and many inhabitants fled higher up into the mountains and out of their settlements. Traditionally Catholic and part of the Holy Roman Empire, Protestantism was deemed a threat. Yet many were reforming or converting during this period, and now the majority of the population in the Engadin are Protestant.

The content – perhaps impacted by the First World War – is subjected throughout to contemporary ideology and morality and can thus be read as an interesting cultural document of the 1920s. What is more interesting and impressive, however, is that Rosa Saluz was motivated and brave enough to concern herself with a historical and political subject, as opposed to the private or poetic as readers in the 1920s would likely have expected of a woman.

The story starts and ends in Gonda, a village in the Engadin between Lavin and Guarda, first mentioned in the year 1161, and now only a mediaeval ruin. The Protestant chronicler Ulrich Campell (Duri Chiampell) mentions the settlement in Lavin in his *Raetiae alpestris topographica descriptio* from 1570. He speaks of approximately thirty buildings. In 1741, Nicolin Sererhard describes the village as uninhabited and abandoned in *Einfalte Delineation aller Gemeinden gemeiner dreien Bünden*. The inhabitants were most likely driven out by avalanches, floods and the economic situation, but also by the invasion of the Catholic-Austrian general, Alois Baldiron.

Gonda: utopia and hometown of the beautiful young Catholic, Cilgia Enzio, a typical Engadin girl, and the strong and courageous young Protestant, Martin Massol, both with 'black eyes', fated for one another. The girl is always described as wearing traditional Engadin garb with a big amber necklace. Rosa Saluz recounts the legend and describes all characters as having a 'patriotic accent'. The garb in this context is a clear statement: it says 'here the housewife, at home in traditional garb'; 'there the man in uniform going to war to protect his homeland and avenge their ancestors'. The marriage between Cilgia and Martin is only possible once Cilgia sees the massacred Protestants in Valtellina and decides to convert.

To respond a hundred years later to her message, style and vocabulary is not easy, but it is a challenge that inspired me and which I have attempted here three times.

THE FIRST ATTEMPT
taken from this quip from Rosa Saluz's story:

Sunshine all the time would be too bright,
Clear skies all the time would be trouble,
Rain and snow are needed too,
If you want to enjoy the sun double!

This brand of wisdom is encouraging for an individual or a collective in times of crisis (or maybe at any time), and it has gained new relevance in the final months of 2020, under the label 'Sufficiency'. It has gained new relevance thanks to the fervour around climate change and ecology, and subsequently thanks to the Covid-19 pandemic with its social isolation and all the restrictions and consequences that have come with it, including the economic. At least to start with, people in Switzerland had positive experiences of unexpected solidarity. Before, most of us − in clear contrast with the experiences of our ancestors and evolutional expectations − were used to abundance, even overabundance. This, in combination with our constant rushing around (in fact, precisely because of the combination) puts a lot of stress on a society. That and the loss of a metaphysical aspect, perhaps.

On the WWF website, a heading reads 'Sufficiency: Less is More'. You can read that we produce 730 kilos of rubbish per person per year, we let on average 110 kilos of good food go to waste and we release more than two tonnes of CO_2 into the atmosphere just from going on holiday. Under the label 'Sufficiency', various ideas are being gathered on how humans can be just as happy or even happier if we used fewer resources. Most of us Swiss have more than enough. We have so much that essential and existential things, like gratitude and humility, things that generate happiness, are no longer at the centre of our attention.

Is less really more? If you observe the value that a period of relative austerity adds to a day of celebration, you have to say yes.

How good that first beer tastes compared to the seventh! How much better the Sunday roast tastes if you haven't been stuffed with roasts all week.

Thoughts not on the Grisons Turmoil, but on Grisons luxury.

A SECOND REACTION

on reading sentences from *Las chasas* da Gonda

The soft breeze has become wind.

The horminum pyrenaicum that sleep in the bosom of the earth have been dug up with a digger to build a spa with a gym and a Japanese restaurant.

The goddess of spring arrived on a path across the field and there she met three patients from the holistic clinic in Susch where people with burnout are rekindled.

Only the Inn murmurs its solemn nocturnal song. You can still hear the River Inn at night, but during the day – at least during high season in the Upper Engadin – private jets roar across the sky past the Lower Engadin. It's not only the locals, the Franco-Venetians and the Spanish-Habsburgs who are here, it's everyone. Whether that is the reason the Inn's song is now more solemn, I couldn't say.

While washing... a deep sigh escapes from his chest; his gaze full of fervent yearning is directed upwards towards the mountains. His phone was dead and he didn't have a portable charger.

It's no longer *the people of Grisons*, but the population.

Betraying the homeland. This is no longer possible. Today, you betray your partner, whose WhatsApp you checked to see who they are messaging at two in the morning.

A THIRD POINT

Rosa Saluz used the surname 'Enzio' in her story (Cilgia, Tina and Domenicus Enzio), which she discovered in the writing of the Susch chronicler, Ulrich Campell, an ancestor of my husband. In a later edition of his work, titled *Rhaetian History*, he refers to a family from Gonda in the sixteenth century who were apparently known by the name Rapicier (from the Latin 'rapa', white turnip, which was on their crest). Rosa Saluz describes a 'carrot as their emblem' and the footnote explains that it is a 'long root'; both are wrong.

Campell writes 'Entzio' with a 't', which is the Latinised form of 'von Zun'. In the *Historical-Biographical Encyclopaedia of Switzerland*, under 'Vonzun' you can find the variations 'Enzun' and 'Azun', from 'à Zun' (like the common Engadin names à Porta and à Planta). The name Vonzun still exists today, as does Fanzun, and it still has a white turnip on its crest. 'Gianzun' also derives from 'Zun', most likely the composition of a first name and surname, Gian and Zun. Gianzun was Italianised in the seventeenth century to Ganzoni.

In Saluz's story, an Enzio and a Vonzun are married. A Zun with a Zun. A Zun and a Zun, redoubled. Zun squared. Then here, a hundred years later, a Ganzoni holds the texts in her hands. What a small world.

Romana Ganzoni's *Blackboard* is a collection of short reflections on her own life, including childhood memories, notes on Alpine life, and commentaries on current local affairs. It was first published in Switzerland's fourth national language, Romansh. This minority language is spoken in the Canton of Grisons in eastern Switzerland, where most of Ganzoni's short pieces take place. More specifically, it was written in the Romansh dialect of the Lower Engadin, Vallader.

Ganzoni takes the reader on a journey through the Engadin valley and highlights its complex multilingual culture through her language choices. Language is incredibly important in Ganzoni's work, as she manoeuvres between Romansh and its multiple dialects, its dominant, neighbours German and Italian, as well as the other official Swiss language, French, and the global language, English. In 'Shopping List: Three Apples', she mentions both the dialects spoken in the Engadin valley, Vallader and Puter, referring to the different words for apple, 'mail' and 'pom', not at all similar in sound. Another of the more challenging elements to translate in Ganzoni's work was the subtle linguistic and cultural references she makes, which she provides without any context for the reader. A couple of examples are *The Box of Six Wonders*, a local fairy tale, and *The Buildings of Gonda*, a piece of historic Romansh literature.

In these pieces, not only does Ganzoni take the reader through an exploration of language and culture, she also takes us to different locations across Europe, where she subtly brings up questions that plague both the local and global communities. Ganzoni does this by using fantastical references that spring from observations, trains of thought, memories or other words. For example, citing Rosa Saluz's *Las chasas da Gonda* in the final text, '*Patriotism and Sufficiency*', Ganzoni reflects on how the area has changed in the last century from a rural valley to a wealthy tourist destination, thus highlighting the stark contrast between the two, but also commenting on consumerism and the recent fervour for more ecological choices. Consumerism and poverty are also subjects in several other texts, including 'Rosy Cheeks', 'The Trip' and 'Zurich'. My hope in translating this selection of Ganzoni's writing was that their local specificity would bring the English reader closer to the complexities of the history, culture and languages of the Engadin Valley.

+SVIZRA is a series of eight chapbooks showcasing contemporary writing translated from the four official languages of Switzerland: German, French, Italian and Romansh. In giving equal visibility to each of the four languages, **+SVIZRA** offers a range of Swiss writing never before seen in English from a diverse group of some of the best authors living and working in Switzerland today, including National Literature Prize winning Anna Ruchat, Iraqi exile Usama Al-Shahmani and treasured Romansh author, Rut Plouda.

+SVIZRA is the result of Strangers Press' latest exciting collaboration with an international group of authors, translators, publishers, designers and editors, all made possible by generous funding from Pro Helvetia.

Supported By

University of East Anglia

NORWICH
UNIVERSITY
OF THE ARTS